THE YELLOW WALLPAPER

The author's most highly acclaimed short story.
First published in 1892.

WOMAN

A collection of satirical poems about female inequality in
Gilman's time.
Woman *forms the second part of the*
*trilogy of poems in **In This Our World**.*
First published in 1893.

Charlotte Perkins Gilman

First published 2015
Copyright © 2015 Aziloth Books

British Library Cataloguing in Publication Data

A catalogue record for this book is available from the British Library.

ISBN-13: 978-1-909735-88-0
Printed and bound in Great Britain by Lightning Source UK Ltd., 6 Precedent Drive, Rooksley, Milton Keynes MK13 8PR.

Front cover Illustration: Aziloth Books, © 2015

CONTENTS

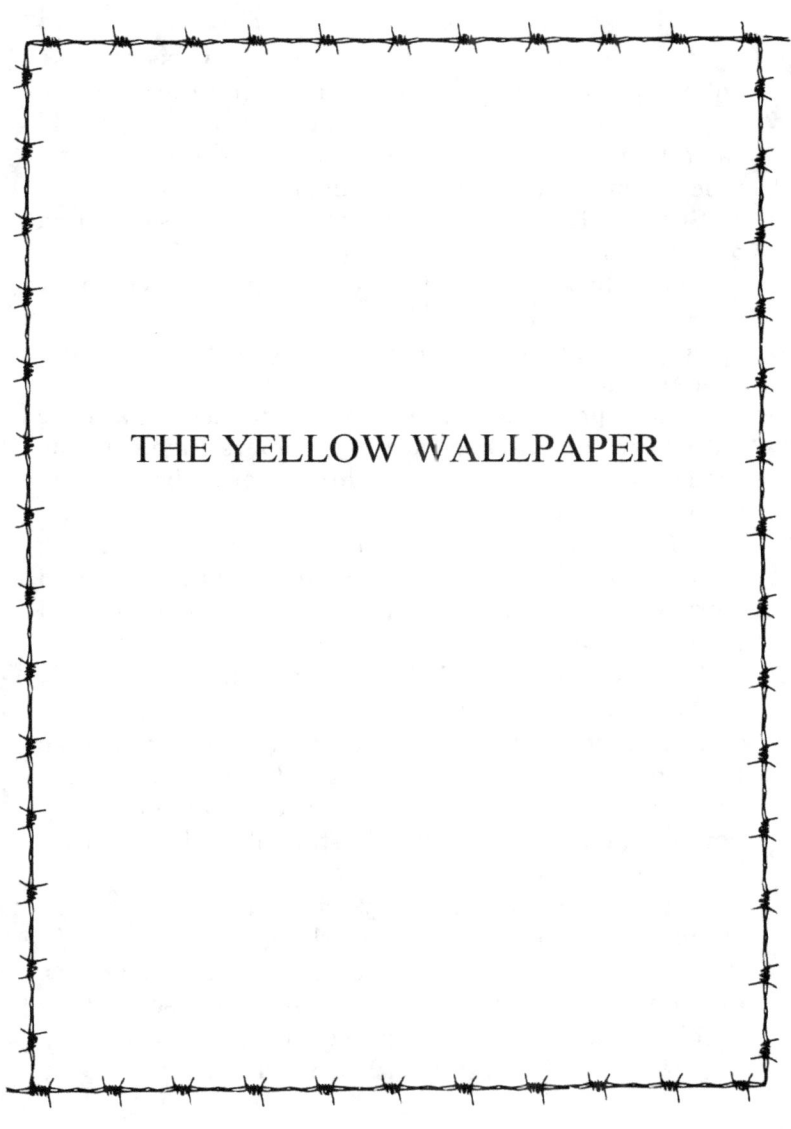

THE YELLOW WALLPAPER

It is very seldom that mere ordinary people like John and myself secure ancestral halls for the summer.

A colonial mansion, a hereditary estate, I would say a haunted house, and reach the height of romantic felicity - but that would be asking too much of fate!

Still I will proudly declare that there is something queer about it.

Else, why should it be let so cheaply? And why have stood so long untenanted?

John laughs at me, of course, but one expects that in marriage.

John is practical in the extreme. He has no patience with faith, an intense horror of superstition, and he scoffs openly at any talk of things not to be felt and seen and put down in figures.

John is a physician, and *perhaps* - (I would not say it to a living soul, of course, but this is dead paper and a great relief to my mind) - *perhaps* that is one reason I do not get well faster.

You see he does not believe I am sick!

And what can one do?

If a physician of high standing, and one's own husband, assures friends and relatives that there is really nothing the matter with one but temporary nervous depression - a slight hysterical tendency - what is one to do?

My brother is also a physician, and also of high standing, and he says the same thing.

So I take phosphates or phosphites - whichever it is, and tonics, and journeys, and air, and exercise, and am absolutely forbidden to "work" until I am well again.

Personally, I disagree with their ideas.

Personally, I believe that congenial work, with excitement and change, would do me good.

But what is one to do?

I did write for a while in spite of them; but it *does* exhaust me a good deal - having to be so sly about it, or else meet with heavy opposition.

I sometimes fancy that in my condition if I had less opposition and more society and stimulus - but John says the very worst thing I can do is to think about my condition, and I confess it always makes me feel bad.

So I will let it alone and talk about the house.

The most beautiful place! It is quite alone, standing well back from the road, quite three miles from the village. It makes me think of English places that you read about, for there are hedges and walls and gates that lock, and lots of separate little houses for the gardeners and people.

There is a *delicious* garden! I never saw such a garden - large and shady, full of box-bordered paths, and lined with long grape-covered arbors with seats under them.

There were greenhouses, too, but they are all broken now.

There was some legal trouble, I believe, something about the heirs and coheirs; anyhow, the place has been empty for years.

That spoils my ghostliness, I am afraid, but I don't care - there is something strange about the house - I can feel it.

I even said so to John one moonlight evening, but he said what I felt was a *draught*, and shut the window.

I get unreasonably angry with John sometimes. I'm sure I never used to be so sensitive. I think it is due to this nervous condition.

But John says if I feel so, I shall neglect proper self-control; so I take pains to control myself - before him, at least, and that makes me very tired.

I don't like our room a bit. I wanted one downstairs that opened on the piazza and had roses all over the window, and such pretty old-fashioned chintz hangings! but John would not hear of it.

He said there was only one window and not room for two beds, and no near room for him if he took another.

He is very careful and loving, and hardly lets me stir without special direction.

I have a schedule prescription for each hour in the day; he takes all care from me, and so I feel basely ungrateful not to value it more.

He said we came here solely on my account, that I was to have perfect rest and all the air I could get. "Your exercise depends on your strength, my dear," said he, "and your food somewhat on your appetite; but air you can absorb all the time." So we took the nursery at the top of the house.

It is a big, airy room, the whole floor nearly, with windows that look all ways, and air and sunshine galore. It was nursery first and then playroom and gymnasium, I should judge; for the windows are barred for little children, and there are rings and things in the walls.

The paint and paper look as if a boys' school had used it. It is stripped off - the paper - in great patches all around the head of my bed, about as far as I can reach, and in a great place on the other side of the room low down. I never saw a worse paper in my life.

One of those sprawling flamboyant patterns committing every artistic sin.

It is dull enough to confuse the eye in following, pronounced enough to constantly irritate and provoke study, and when you follow the lame uncertain curves for a little distance they suddenly commit suicide - plunge off at outrageous angles, destroy themselves in unheard of contradictions.

The color is repellent, almost revolting; a smouldering unclean yellow, strangely faded by the slow-turning sunlight.

It is a dull yet lurid orange in some places, a sickly sulphur tint in others.

No wonder the children hated it! I should hate it myself if I had to live in this room long.

There comes John, and I must put this away, - he hates to have me write a word

We have been here two weeks, and I haven't felt like writing before, since that first day.

I am sitting by the window now, up in this atrocious nursery, and there is nothing to hinder my writing as much as I please, save lack of strength.

John is away all day, and even some nights when his cases are serious.

I am glad my case is not serious!

But these nervous troubles are dreadfully depressing.

John does not know how much I really suffer. He knows there is no *reason* to suffer, and that satisfies him.

Of course it is only nervousness. It does weigh on me so not to do my duty in any way!

I meant to be such a help to John, such a real rest and

comfort, and here I am a comparative burden already!

Nobody would believe what an effort it is to do what little I am able, - to dress and entertain, and order things.

It is fortunate Mary is so good with the baby. Such a dear baby!

And yet I *cannot* be with him, it makes me so nervous.

I suppose John never was nervous in his life. He laughs at me so about this wall-paper!

At first he meant to repaper the room, but afterwards he said that I was letting it get the better of me, and that nothing was worse for a nervous patient than to give way to such fancies.

He said that after the wall-paper was changed it would be the heavy bedstead, and then the barred windows, and then that gate at the head of the stairs, and so on.

"You know the place is doing you good," he said, "and really, dear, I don't care to renovate the house just for a three months' rental."

"Then do let us go downstairs," I said, "there are such pretty rooms there."

Then he took me in his arms and called me a blessed little goose, and said he would go down to the cellar, if I wished, and have it whitewashed into the bargain.

But he is right enough about the beds and windows and things.

It is an airy and comfortable room as any one need wish, and, of course, I would not be so silly as to make him uncomfortable just for a whim.

I'm really getting quite fond of the big room, all but

that horrid paper.

Out of one window I can see the garden, those mysterious deepshaded arbors, the riotous old-fashioned flowers, and bushes and gnarly trees.

Out of another I get a lovely view of the bay and a little private wharf belonging to the estate. There is a beautiful shaded lane that runs down there from the house. I always fancy I see people walking in these numerous paths and arbors, but John has cautioned me not to give way to fancy in the least. He says that with my imaginative power and habit of story-making, a nervous weakness like mine is sure to lead to all manner of excited fancies, and that I ought to use my will and good sense to check the tendency. So I try.

I think sometimes that if I were only well enough to write a little it would relieve the press of ideas and rest me.

But I find I get pretty tired when I try.

It is so discouraging not to have any advice and companionship about my work. When I get really well, John says we will ask Cousin Henry and Julia down for a long visit; but he says he would as soon put fireworks in my pillow-case as to let me have those stimulating people about now.

I wish I could get well faster.

But I must not think about that. This paper looks to me as if it *knew* what a vicious influence it had!

There is a recurrent spot where the pattern lolls like a broken neck and two bulbous eyes stare at you upside down.

I get positively angry with the impertinence of it and the everlastingness. Up and down and sideways they crawl, and those absurd, unblinking eyes are everywhere. There is one place where two breadths didn't match, and the eyes go all up and down the line, one a little higher than the other.

I never saw so much expression in an inanimate thing before, and we all know how much expression they have! I used to lie awake as a child and get more entertainment and terror out of blank walls and plain furniture than most children could find in a toy store.

I remember what a kindly wink the knobs of our big, old bureau used to have, and there was one chair that always seemed like a strong friend.

I used to feel that if any of the other things looked too fierce I could always hop into that chair and be safe.

The furniture in this room is no worse than inharmonious, however, for we had to bring it all from downstairs. I suppose when this was used as a playroom they had to take the nursery things out, and no wonder! I never saw such ravages as the children have made here.

The wall-paper, as I said before, is torn off in spots, and it sticketh closer than a brother - they must have had perseverance as well as hatred.

Then the floor is scratched and gouged and splintered, the plaster itself is dug out here and there, and this great heavy bed which is all we found in the room, looks as if it had been through the wars.

But I don't mind it a bit - only the paper.

There comes John's sister. Such a dear girl as she is, and so careful of me! I must not let her find me writing.

She is a perfect and enthusiastic housekeeper, and hopes for no better profession. I verily believe she thinks it is the writing which made me sick!

But I can write when she is out, and see her a long way off from these windows.

There is one that commands the road, a lovely shaded winding road, and one that just looks off over the country. A lovely country, too, full of great elms and velvet meadows.

This wall-paper has a kind of sub-pattern in a different shade, a particularly irritating one, for you can only see it in certain lights and not clearly then.

But in the places where it isn't faded and where the sun is just so - I can see a strange, provoking, formless sort of figure, that seems to skulk about behind that silly and conspicuous front design.

There's sister on the stairs!

Well, the Fourth of July is over! The people are gone and I am tired out. John thought it might do me good to see a little company, so we just had mother and Nellie and the children down for a week.

Of course I didn't do a thing. Jennie sees to everything now.

But it tired me all the same.

John says if I don't pick up faster he shall send me to Weir Mitchell in the fall.

But I don't want to go there at all. I had a friend who was in his hands once, and she says he is just like John and my brother, only more so!

Besides, it is such an undertaking to go so far.

I don't feel as if it was worth while to turn my hand over for anything, and I'm getting dreadfully fretful and querulous.

I cry at nothing, and cry most of the time.

Of course I don't when John is here, or anybody else, but when I am alone.

And I am alone a good deal just now. John is kept in town very often by serious cases, and Jennie is good and lets me alone when I want her to.

So I walk a little in the garden or down that lovely lane, sit on the porch under the roses, and lie down up here a good deal.

I'm getting really fond of the room in spite of the wall-paper. Perhaps *because* of the wall-paper.

It dwells in my mind so!

I lie here on this great immovable bed - it is nailed down, I believe - and follow that pattern about by the hour. It is as good as gymnastics, I assure you. I start, we'll say, at the bottom, down in the corner over there where it has not been touched, and I determine for the thousandth time that I *will* follow that pointless pattern to some sort of a conclusion.

I know a little of the principle of design, and I know this thing was not arranged on any laws of radiation, or alternation, or repetition, or symmetry, or anything else that I ever heard of.

It is repeated, of course, by the breadths, but not otherwise.

Looked at in one way each breadth stands alone, the bloated curves and flourishes - a kind of "debased Romanesque" with delirium tremens - go waddling up and down in isolated columns of fatuity.

But, on the other hand, they connect diagonally, and the sprawling outlines run off in great slanting waves of optic horror, like a lot of wallowing seaweeds in full chase.

The whole thing goes horizontally, too, at least it seems so, and I exhaust myself in trying to distinguish the order of its going in that direction.

They have used a horizontal breadth for a frieze, and that adds wonderfully to the confusion.

There is one end of the room where it is almost intact, and there, when the crosslights fade and the low sun shines directly upon it, I can almost fancy radiation after all, - the interminable grotesques seem to form around a common centre and rush off in headlong plunges of equal distraction.

It makes me tired to follow it. I will take a nap I guess.

I don't know why I should write this.

I don't want to.

I don't feel able.

And I know John would think it absurd. But I *must* say what I feel and think in some way - it is such a relief!

But the effort is getting to be greater than the relief.

Half the time now I am awfully lazy, and lie down ever so much.

John says I musn't lose my strength, and has me take cod liver oil and lots of tonics and things, to say nothing of ale and wine and rare meat.

Dear John! He loves me very dearly, and hates to have me sick. I tried to have a real earnest reasonable talk with him the other day, and tell him how I wish he would let me go and make a visit to Cousin Henry and Julia.

But he said I wasn't able to go, nor able to stand it after I got there; and I did not make out a very good case for myself, for I was crying before I had finished.

It is getting to be a great effort for me to think straight. Just this nervous weakness I suppose.

And dear John gathered me up in his arms, and just carried me upstairs and laid me on the bed, and sat by me and read to me till it tired my head.

He said I was his darling and his comfort and all he had, and that I must take care of myself for his sake, and keep well.

He says no one but myself can help me out of it, that I must use my will and self-control and not let any silly fancies run away with me.

There's one comfort, the baby is well and happy, and does not have to occupy this nursery with the horrid wall-paper.

If we had not used it, that blessed child would have! What a fortunate escape! Why, I wouldn't have a child of mine, an impressionable little thing, live in such a room for worlds.

I never thought of it before, but it is lucky that John kept me here after all, I can stand it so much easier than a baby, you see.

Of course I never mention it to them any more - I am too wise, - but I keep watch of it all the same.

There are things in that paper that nobody knows but me, or ever will.

Behind that outside pattern the dim shapes get clearer every day.

It is always the same shape, only very numerous.

And it is like a woman stooping down and creeping about behind that pattern. I don't like it a bit. I wonder - I begin to think - I wish John would take me away from here!

It is so hard to talk with John about my case, because he is so wise, and because he loves me so.

But I tried it last night.

It was moonlight. The moon shines in all around just as the sun does.

I hate to see it sometimes, it creeps so slowly, and always comes in by one window or another.

John was asleep and I hated to waken him, so I kept still and watched the moonlight on that undulating wall-paper till I felt creepy.

The faint figure behind seemed to shake the pattern, just as if she wanted to get out.

I got up softly and went to feel and see if the paper *did* move, and when I came back John was awake.

"What is it, little girl?" he said. "Don't go walking about like that - you'll get cold."

I though it was a good time to talk, so I told him that I really was not gaining here, and that I wished he would take me away.

"Why darling!" said he, "our lease will be up in three weeks, and I can't see how to leave before.

"The repairs are not done at home, and I cannot possibly leave town just now. Of course if you were in any danger, I could and would, but you really are better, dear, whether you can see it or not. I am a doctor, dear, and I know. You are gaining flesh and color, your appetite is better, I feel really much easier about you."

"I don't weigh a bit more," said I, "nor as much; and my appetite may be better in the evening when you are here, but it is worse in the morning when you are away!"

"Bless her little heart!" said he with a big hug, "she

shall be as sick as she pleases! But now let's improve the shining hours by going to sleep, and talk about it in the morning!"

"And you won't go away?" I asked gloomily.

"Why, how can I, dear? It is only three weeks more and then we will take a nice little trip of a few days while Jennie is getting the house ready. Really dear you are better!"

"Better in body perhaps - " I began, and stopped short, for he sat up straight and looked at me with such a stern, reproachful look that I could not say another word.

"My darling," said he, "I beg of you, for my sake and for our child's sake, as well as for your own, that you will never for one instant let that idea enter your mind! There is nothing so dangerous, so fascinating, to a temperament like yours. It is a false and foolish fancy. Can you not trust me as a physician when I tell you so?"

So of course I said no more on that score, and we went to sleep before long. He thought I was asleep first, but I wasn't, and lay there for hours trying to decide whether that front pattern and the back pattern really did move together or separately.

On a pattern like this, by daylight, there is a lack of sequence, a defiance of law, that is a constant irritant to a normal mind.

The color is hideous enough, and unreliable enough, and infuriating enough, but the pattern is torturing.

You think you have mastered it, but just as you get well underway in following, it turns a back-somersault and there you are. It slaps you in the face, knocks you down, and tramples upon you. It is like a bad dream.

The outside pattern is a florid arabesque, reminding one of a fungus. If you can imagine a toadstool in joints, an interminable string of toadstools, budding and sprouting in endless convolutions - why, that is something like it.

That is, sometimes!

There is one marked peculiarity about this paper, a thing nobody seems to notice but myself, and that is that it changes as the light changes.

When the sun shoots in through the east window - I always watch for that first long, straight ray - it changes so quickly that I never can quite believe it.

That is why I watch it always.

By moonlight - the moon shines in all night when there is a moon - I wouldn't know it was the same paper.

At night in any kind of light, in twilight, candle light, lamplight, and worst of all by moonlight, it becomes bars! The outside pattern I mean, and the woman behind it is as plain as can be.

I didn't realize for a long time what the thing was that showed behind, that dim sub-pattern, but now I am quite sure it is a woman.

By daylight she is subdued, quiet. I fancy it is the pattern that keeps her so still. It is so puzzling. It keeps me quiet by the hour.

I lie down ever so much now. John says it is good for me, and to sleep all I can.

Indeed he started the habit by making me lie down for an hour after each meal.

It is a very bad habit I am convinced, for you see I don't sleep.

And that cultivates deceit, for I don't tell them I'm awake - O no!

The fact is I am getting a little afraid of John.

He seems very queer sometimes, and even Jennie has an inexplicable look.

It strikes me occasionally, just as a scientific hypothesis, - that perhaps it is the paper!

I have watched John when he did not know I was looking, and come into the room suddenly on the most innocent excuses, and I've caught him several times *looking at the paper*! And Jennie too. I caught Jennie with her hand on it once.

She didn't know I was in the room, and when I asked her in a quiet, a very quiet voice, with the most restrained manner possible, what she was doing with the paper - she turned around as if she had been caught stealing, and looked quite angry - asked me why I should frighten her so!

Then she said that the paper stained everything it touched, that she had found yellow smooches on all my clothes and John's, and she wished we would be more careful!

Did not that sound innocent? But I know she was studying that pattern, and I am determined that nobody shall find it out but myself!

Life is very much more exciting now than it used to be. You see I have something more to expect, to look forward to, to watch. I really do eat better, and am more quiet than I was.

John is so pleased to see me improve! He laughed a little the other day, and said I seemed to be flourishing in spite of my wall-paper.

I turned it off with a laugh. I had no intention of telling him it was *because* of the wall-paper - he would make fun of me. He might even want to take me away.

I don't want to leave now until I have found it out. There is a week more, and I think that will be enough.

I'm feeling ever so much better! I don't sleep much at night, for it is so interesting to watch developments; but I sleep a good deal in the daytime.

In the daytime it is tiresome and perplexing.

There are always new shoots on the fungus, and new shades of yellow all over it. I cannot keep count of them, though I have tried conscientiously.

It is the strangest yellow, that wall-paper! It makes me think of all the yellow things I ever saw - not beautiful ones like buttercups, but old foul, bad yellow things.

But there is something else about that paper - the smell! I noticed it the moment we came into the room, but with so much air and sun it was not bad. Now we have had a week of fog and rain, and whether the windows are open or not, the smell is here.

It creeps all over the house.

I find it hovering in the dining-room, skulking in the parlor, hiding in the hall, lying in wait for me on the stairs.

It gets into my hair.

Even when I go to ride, if I turn my head suddenly and surprise it - there is that smell!

Such a peculiar odor, too! I have spent hours in trying to analyze it, to find what it smelled like.

It is not bad - at first, and very gentle, but quite the subtlest, most enduring odor I ever met.

In this damp weather it is awful, I wake up in the night and find it hanging over me.

It used to disturb me at first. I thought seriously of burning the house - to reach the smell.

But now I am used to it. The only thing I can think of that it is like is the *color* of the paper! A yellow smell.

There is a very funny mark on this wall, low down, near the mopboard. A streak that runs round the room. It goes behind every piece of furniture, except the bed, a long, straight, even *smooch*, as if it had been rubbed over and over.

I wonder how it was done and who did it, and what they did it for. Round and round and round - round and round and round - it makes me dizzy!

I really have discovered something at last.

Through watching so much at night, when it changes so, I have finally found out.

The front pattern *does* move - and no wonder! The woman behind shakes it!

Sometimes I think there are a great many women behind, and sometimes only one, and she crawls around fast, and her crawling shakes it all over.

Then in the very bright spots she keeps still, and in the very shady spots she just takes hold of the bars and shakes them hard.

And she is all the time trying to climb through. But nobody could climb through that pattern - it strangles so; I think that is why it has so many heads.

They get through, and then the pattern strangles them off and turns them upside down, and makes their eyes white!

If those heads were covered or taken off it would not be half so bad.

I think that woman gets out in the daytime!

And I'll tell you why - privately - I've seen her!

I can see her out of every one of my windows!

It is the same woman, I know, for she is always creeping, and most women do not creep by daylight.

I see her on that long road under the trees, creeping along, and when a carriage comes she hides under the blackberry vines.

I don't blame her a bit. It must be very humiliating to be caught creeping by daylight!

I always lock the door when I creep by daylight. I can't do it at night, for I know John would suspect something at once.

And John is so queer now, that I don't want to irritate him. I wish he would take another room! Besides, I don't want anybody to get that woman out at night but myself.

I often wonder if I could see her out of all the windows at once.

But, turn as fast as I can, I can only see out of one at one time.

And though I always see her, she *may* be able to creep faster than I can turn!

I have watched her sometimes away off in the open country, creeping as fast as a cloud shadow in a high wind.

If only that top pattern could be gotten off from the under one! I mean to try it, little by little.

I have found out another funny thing, but I shan't tell it this time! It does not do to trust people too much.

There are only two more days to get this paper off, and I believe John is beginning to notice. I don't like the look in his eyes.

And I heard him ask Jennie a lot of professional questions about me. She had a very good report to give.

She said I slept a good deal in the daytime.

John knows I don't sleep very well at night, for all I'm so quiet!

He asked me all sorts of questions, too, and pretended to be very loving and kind.

As if I couldn't see through him!

Still, I don't wonder he acts so, sleeping under this paper for three months.

It only interests me, but I feel sure John and Jennie are secretly affected by it.

Hurrah! This is the last day, but it is enough. John is to stay in town over night, and won't be out until this evening.

Jennie wanted to sleep with me - the sly thing! but I told her I should undoubtedly rest better for a night all alone.

That was clever, for really I wasn't alone a bit! As soon as it was moonlight and that poor thing began to crawl and shake the pattern, I got up and ran to help her.

I pulled and she shook, I shook and she pulled, and before morning we had peeled off yards of that paper.

A strip about as high as my head and half around the room.

And then when the sun came and that awful pattern began to laugh at me, I declared I would finish it to-day!

We go away to-morrow, and they are moving all my furniture down again to leave things as they were before.

Jennie looked at the wall in amazement, but I told

her merrily that I did it out of pure spite at the vicious thing.

She laughed and said she wouldn't mind doing it herself, but I must not get tired.

How she betrayed herself that time!

But I am here, and no person touches this paper but me - not *alive*!

She tried to get me out of the room - it was too patent! But I said it was so quiet and empty and clean now that I believed I would lie down again and sleep all I could; and not to wake me even for dinner - I would call when I woke.

So now she is gone, and the servants are gone, and the things are gone, and there is nothing left but that great bedstead nailed down, with the canvas mattress we found on it.

We shall sleep downstairs to-night, and take the boat home to-morrow.

I quite enjoy the room, now it is bare again.

How those children did tear about here!

This bedstead is fairly gnawed!

But I must get to work.

I have locked the door and thrown the key down into the front path.

I don't want to go out, and I don't want to have anybody come in, till John comes.

I want to astonish him.

I've got a rope up here that even Jennie did not find. If that woman does get out, and tries to get away, I can tie her!

But I forgot I could not reach far without anything to stand on!

This bed will *not* move!

I tried to lift and push it until I was lame, and then I got so angry I bit off a little piece at one corner - but it hurt my teeth.

Then I peeled off all the paper I could reach standing on the floor. It sticks horribly and the pattern just enjoys it! All those strangled heads and bulbous eyes and waddling fungus growths just shriek with derision!

I am getting angry enough to do something desperate. To jump out of the window would be admirable exercise, but the bars are too strong even to try.

Besides I wouldn't do it. Of course not. I know well enough that a step like that is improper and might be misconstrued.

I don't like to *look* out of the windows even - there are so many of those creeping women, and they creep so fast.

I wonder if they all come out of that wall-paper as I did?

But I am securely fastened now by my well-hidden rope - you don't get *me* out in the road there!

I suppose I shall have to get back behind the pattern when it comes night, and that is hard!

It is so pleasant to be out in this great room and creep around as I please!

I don't want to go outside. I won't, even if Jennie asks me to.

For outside you have to creep on the ground, and everything is green instead of yellow.

But here I can creep smoothly on the floor, and my shoulder just fits in that long smooch around the wall, so I cannot lose my way.

Why there's John at the door!

It is no use, young man, you can't open it!

How he does call and pound!

Now he's crying for an axe.

It would be a shame to break down that beautiful door!

"John dear!" said I in the gentlest voice, "the key is down by the front steps, under a plantain leaf!"

That silenced him for a few moments.

Then he said - very quietly indeed, "Open the door, my darling!"

"I can't," said I. "The key is down by the front door under a plantain leaf!"

And then I said it again, several times, very gently and slowly, and said it so often that he had to go and see, and he got it of course, and came in. He stopped short by the door.

"What is the matter?" he cried. "For God's sake, what are you doing!"

I kept on creeping just the same, but I looked at him over my shoulder.

"I've got out at last," said I, "in spite of you and Jane. And I've pulled off most of the paper, so you can't put me back!"

Now why should that man have fainted? But he did, and right across my path by the wall, so that I had to creep over him every time!

WOMAN

SHE WALKETH VEILED AND SLEEPING

She walketh veiled and sleeping,
For she knoweth not her power;
She obeyeth but the pleading
Of her heart, and the high leading
Of her soul, unto this hour.
Slow advancing, halting, creeping,
Comes the Woman to the hour! -
She walketh veiled and sleeping.
For she knoweth not her power.

TO MAN

In dark and early ages, through the primal forests
  faring,
Ere the soul came shining into prehistoric night,
Two-fold man was equal; they were comrades dear
  and daring.
Living wild and free together in unreasoning delight.

Ere the soul was born and consciousness came
  slowly,
Ere the soul was born, to man and woman too.
Ere he found the Tree of Knowledge, that awful
  tree and holy.
Ere he knew he felt, and knew he knew.

Then said he to Pain, " I am wise now, and I know
  you!

No more will I suffer while power and wisdom
    last!"
Then said he to Pleasure, "I am strong, and I will
    show you
That the will of man can seize you; aye, and hold
    you fast!"

Food he ate for pleasure, and wine he drank for
    gladness,
And woman? Ah, the woman! the crown of all
    delight! -
His now - he knew it! He was strong to madness
In that early dawning after prehistoric night.
His - his forever! That glory sweet and tender!
Ah, but he would love her! And she should love
    but him!
He would work and struggle for her, he would
    shelter and defend her;
She should never leave him, never, till their eyes
    in death were dim.

Close, close he bound her, that she should leave
    him never;
Weak still he kept her, lest she be strong to flee;
And the fainting flame of passion he kept alive
    forever
With all the arts and forces of earth and sky and sea.
And, ah, the long journey! The slow and awful
    ages
They have labored up together, blind and crippled,
    all astray!
Through what a mighty volume, with a million
    shameful pages,
From the freedom of the forest to the prisons of
    to-day!

Food he ate for pleasure, and it slew him with
    diseases!
Wine he drank for gladness, and it led the way to
    crime!
And woman? He will hold her - he will have
    her when he pleases -
And he never once hath seen her since the pre-
    historic time!

Gone the friend and comrade of the day when life
    was younger,
She who rests and comforts, she who helps and
    saves;
Still he seeks her vainly, with a never-dying
    hunger;
Alone beneath his tyrants, alone above his slaves!

Toiler, bent and weary with the load of thine own
    making!
Thou who art sad and lonely, though lonely all in
    vain!
Who hast sought to conquer Pleasure and have her
    for the taking,
And found that Pleasure only was another name
    for Pain, -

Nature hath reclaimed thee, forgiving dispossession!
God hath not forgotten, though man doth still for-
    get!
The woman-soul is rising, in despite of thy trans-
    gression;
Loose her now - and trust her! She will love thee
    yet!

Love thee? She will love thee as only freedom
    knoweth;
Love thee? She will love thee while Love itself
    doth live!
Fear not the heart of woman! No bitterness it
    showeth!
The ages of her sorrow have but taught her to
    forgive!

WOMEN OF TO-DAY

You women of today who fear so much
The women of the future, showing how
The dangers of her course are such and such -
       What are you now?

Mothers and Wives and Housekeepers, forsooth!
Great names! you cry, full scope to rule and please!
Room for wise age and energetic youth! -
       But are you these?

Housekeepers? Do you then, like those of yore,
Keep house with power and pride, with grace and
    ease?
No, you keep servants only! What is more,
       You don't keep these!
Wives, say you Wives! Blessed indeed are they
Who hold of love the everlasting keys.

Keeping their husbands' hearts! Alas the day!
    You don't keep these!

And mothers? Pitying Heaven! Mark the cry
From cradle death-beds! Mothers on their knees!
Why, half the children born - as children die!
    You don't keep these!

And still the wailing babies come and go,
And homes are waste, and husbands' hearts fly far,
There is no hope until you dare to know
    The thing you are!

TO THE YOUNG WIFE

Are you content, you pretty three-years' wife?
    Are you content and satisfied to live
    On what your loving husband loves to give,
    And give to him your life?

Are you content with work, - to toil alone,
    To clean things dirty and to soil things clean;
    To be a kitchen-maid, be called a queen, -
    Queen of a cook-stove throne?

Are you content to reign in that small space -
    A wooden palace and a yard-fenced land -
    With other queens abundant on each hand,
    Each fastened in her place?

Are you content to rear your children so?
　　Untaught yourself, untrained, perplexed, dis-
　　　　tressed.
　　Are you so sure your way is always best?
　　　　That you can always know?

Have you forgotten how you used to long
　　In days of ardent girlhood, to be great,
　　To help the groaning world, to serve the state,
　　　　To be so wise - so strong?

And are you quite convinced this is the way.
　　The only way a woman's duty lies -
　　Knowing all women so have shut their eyes?
　　　　Seeing the world to-day?

Have you no dream of life in fuller store?
　　Of growing to be more than that you are?
　　Doing the things you now do better far.
　　　　Yet doing others - more?

Losing no love, but finding as you grew
　　That as you entered upon nobler life
　　You so became a richer, sweeter wife,
　　　　A wiser mother too?

What holds you? Ah, my dear, it is your throne,
　　Your paltry queenship in that narrow place,

Your antique labors, your restricted space.
　　　　Your working all alone!
Be not deceived! 'Tis not your wifely bond
That holds you, nor the mother's royal power,

But selfish, slavish service hour by hour -
    A life with no beyond!'

FALSE PLAY

"Do you love me?" asked the mother of her child.
    And the baby answered, "No!"
Great Love listened and sadly smiled;
He knew the love in the heart of the child -
    That you could not wake it so.

"Do not love me?" the foolish mother cried.
    And the baby answered, "No!"
He knew the worth of the trick she tried -
Great Love listened, and grieving, sighed
    That the mother scorned him so.

"Oh, poor mama!" and she played her part
    Till the baby's strength gave way:
He knew it was false in his inmost heart,
But he could not bear that her tears should start,
    So he joined in the lying play.

"Then love mama!" and the soft lips crept
    To the kiss that his love should show, -
The mouth to speak while the spirit slept!
Great Love listened, and blushed, and wept
    That they blasphemed him so.

MOTHERHOOD

MOTHERHOOD: First mere laying of an egg,
With blind foreseeing of the wisest place,
And blind provision of the proper food
For unseen larva to grow fat upon
After the instinct-guided mother died, -
Posthumous motherhood, no love, no joy.

MOTHERHOOD: Brooding patient o'er the nest,
With gentle stirring of an unknown love;
Defending eggs unhatched, feeding the young
For days of callow feebleness, and then
Driving the fledglings from the nest to fly.

MOTHERHOOD: When the kitten and the cub
Cried out alive, and first the mother knew
The fumbling of furry little paws,
The pressure of the hungry little mouths
Against the more than ready mother-breast, -
The love that comes of giving and of care.

MOTHERHOOD: Nursing with her heart-warm milk,
Fighting to death all danger to her young,
Hunting for food for little ones half-weaned.
Teaching them how to hunt and fight in turn, -
Then loving not till the new litter came.

MOTHERHOOD: When the little savage grew
Tall at his mother's side, and learned to feel
Some mother even in his father's heart,
Love coming to new babies while the first

Still needed mother's care, and therefore love, -
Love lasting longer because childhood did.

MOTHERHOOD: Semi-civilized, intense.
Fierce with brute passion, narrow with the range
Of slavish lives to meanest service bowed;
Devoted - to the sacrifice of life;
Jealous beyond belief, and ignorant
Even of what should keep the child alive.
Love spreading with the spread of human needs,
The child's new, changing, ever-growing wants,
Yet seeking like brute mothers of the past
To give all things to her own child herself.
Loving to the exclusion of all else;
To the child's service bending a whole life;
Yet stunting the young creature day by day
With lack of Justice, Liberty, and Peace.

MOTHERHOOD: Civilized. There stands at last,
Facing the heavens with as calm a smile.
The highest fruit of the long work of God;
The highest type of this, the highest race;
She from whose groping instinct grew all love -
All love - in which is all the life of man.
MOTHERHOOD: Seeing with her clear, kind eyes,
Luminous, tender eyes, wherein the smile
Is like the smile of sunlight on the sea.
That the new children of the newer day
Need more than any single heart can give.
More than is known to any single mind,
More than is found in any single house,
And need it from the day they see the light.

Then, measuring her love by what they need,
Gives, from the heart of modern motherhood.
Gives first, as tree to bear God's highest fruit,
A clean, strong body, perfect and full grown,
Fair for the purpose of its womanhood,
Not for light fancy of a lower mind;
Gives a clear mind, athletic, beautiful,
Dispassionate, unswerving from the truth;
Gives a great heart that throbs with human love,
As she would wish her son to love the world.
Then, when the child comes, lovely as a star,
She, in the peace of primal motherhood,
Nurses her baby with unceasing joy,
With milk of human kindness, human health,
Bright human beauty, and immortal love.
And then? Ah! here is the New Motherhood -
The motherhood of the fair new-made world -
O glorious New Mother of New Men!
Her child, with other children from its birth,
In the unstinted freedom of warm air,
Under the wisest eyes, the tenderest thought,
Surrounded by all beauty and all peace.
Led, playing, through the gardens of the world,
With the crowned heads of science and great love
Mapping safe paths for those small, rosy feet, -
Taught human love by feeling human love,
Taught justice by the laws that rule his days,
Taught wisdom by the way in which he lives,
Taught to love all mankind and serve them fair
By seeing, from his birth, all children served
With the same righteous, all-embracing care.
O Mother! Noble Mother, yet to come!

How shall thy child point to the bright career
Of her of whom he boasts to be the son -
Not for assiduous service spent on him.
But for the wisdom which has set him forth
A clear-brained, pure-souled, noble-hearted man,
With health and strength and beauty his by birth;
And, more, for the wide record of her life,
Great work, well done, that makes him praise her
    name
And long to make as great a one his own!
And how shall all the children of the world,
Feeling all mothers love them, loving all.
Rise up and call her blessed!
        This shall be.

SIX HOURS A DAY

Six hours a day the woman spends on food!
Six mortal hours a day
With fire and water toiling, heat and cold;
Struggling with laws she does not understand
Of chemistry and physics, and the weight
Of poverty and ignorance besides.
Toiling for those she loves, the added strain
Of tense emotion on her humble skill,
The sensitiveness born of love and fear,
Making it harder to do even work.
Toiling without release, no hope ahead
Of taking up another business soon.

Of varying the task she finds too hard -
This, her career, so closely interknit
With holier demands as deep as life
That to refuse to cook is held the same
As to refuse her wife and motherhood.
Six mortal hours a day to handle food, -
Prepare it, serve it, clean it all away, -
With allied labors of the stove and tub,
The pan, the dishcloth, and the scrubbing-brush.
Developing forever in her brain
The power to do this work in which she lives;
While the slow finger of Heredity
Writes on the forehead of each living man,
Strive as he may, "His mother was a cook!"

AN OLD PROVERB

"As much pity to see a woman weep as to see a goose go
barefoot."

No escape, little creature! The earth hath no place
For the woman who seeketh to fly from her race.
Poor, ignorant, timid, too helpless to roam,
The woman must bear what befalls her, at home.
Bear bravely, bear dumbly - it is but the same
That all others endure who live under the name.
No escape, little creature!

No escape under heaven! Can man treat you worse

After God has laid on you his infinite curse?
The heaviest burden of sorrow you win
Cannot weigh with the load of original sin;
No shame be too black for the cowering face
Of her who brought shame to the whole human race! -
No escape under heaven!

Yet you feel, being human. You shrink from the
pain
That each child, born a woman, most suffer again.
From the strongest of bonds heart can feel, man
can shape,
You cannot rebel, or appeal, or escape.
You must bear and endure. If the heart cannot
sleep,
And the pain groweth bitter, - too bitter, - then
weep!
For you feel, being human.
And she wept, being woman. The numberless
years
Have counted her burdens and counted her tears;
The maid wept forsaken, the mother forlorn
For the child that was dead, and the child that was
born.
Wept for joy - as a miracle! - wept in her pain!
Wept aloud, wept in secret, wept ever in vain!
Still she weeps, being woman.

REASSURANCE

Can you imagine nothing better, brother,
Than that which you have always had before?
Have you been so content with "wife and mother,"
    You dare hope nothing more?

Have you forever prized her, praised her, sung her,
The happy queen of a most happy reign?
Never dishonored her, despised her, flung her
    Derision and disdain?

Go ask the literature of all the ages!
Books that were written before women read!
Pagan and Christian, satirists and sages, -
    Read what the world has said!

There was no power on earth to bid you slacken
The generous hand that painted her disgrace!
There was no shame on earth too black to blacken
    That much praised woman-face!

Eve and Pandora! - always you begin it -
The ancients called her Sin and Shame and Death!
"There is no evil without woman in it,"
    The modern proverb saith!

She has been yours in uttermost possession, -
Your slave, your mother, your well-chosen bride, -
And you have owned, in million-fold confession,
    You were not satisfied.

Peace, then! Fear not the coming woman, brother!
Owning herself, she giveth all the more!
She shall be better woman, wife, and mother
   Than man hath known before!

MOTHER TO CHILD

How best can I serve thee, my child! My child!
Flesh of my flesh and dear heart of my heart!
Once thou wast within me - I held thee - I fed
   thee -
By the force of my loving and longing I led thee -
   Now we are apart!

I may blind thee with kisses and crush with em-
   bracing,
Thy warm mouth in my neck and our arms inter-
   lacing;
But here in my body my soul lives alone,
And thou answerest me from a house of thine own, -
   That house which I builded!

Which we builded together, thy father and I;
In which thou must live, O my darling, and die!
Not one stone can I alter, one atom relay, -
Not to save or defend thee or help thee to stay -
   That gift is completed!

How best can I serve thee? O child, if they knew
How my heart aches with loving! How deep and
   how true,

How brave and enduring, how patient, how strong,
How longing for good and how fearful of wrong,
   Is the love of thy mother!

Could I crown thee with riches! Surround, over -
   flow thee
With fame and with power till the whole world
   should know thee;
With wisdom and genius to hold the world still,
To bring laughter and tears, joy and pain, at thy will,
Still - *thou* mightst not be happy!

Such have lived - and in sorrow. The greater the
   mind,
The wider and deeper the grief it can find.
The richer, the gladder, the more thou canst feel
The keen stings that a lifetime is sure to reveal.
   O my child! Must thou suffer?

Is there no way my life can save thine from a pain?
Is the love of a mother no possible gain?
No labor of Hercules - search for the Grail -
No way for this wonderful love to avail?
   God in Heaven - O teach me!

My prayer has been answered. The pain thou must
   bear
Is the pain of the world's life which thy life must
   share.
Thou art one with the world - though I love thee
   the best
And to save thee from pain I must save all the rest -
   Well - with God's help I'll do it!

Thou art one with the rest. I must love thee in them.
Thou wilt sin with the rest; and thy mother must
    stem
The world's sin. Thou wilt weep; and thy mother
    must dry
The tears of the world lest her darling should cry.
    I will do it - God helping!

And I stand not alone. I will gather a band
Of all loving mothers from land unto land.
Our children are part of the world! do ye hear?
They are one with the world - we must hold them
    all dear!
    Love all for the child's sake!

For the sake of my child I must hasten to save
All the children on earth from the jail and the grave.
For so, and so only, I lighten the share
Of the pain of the world that my darling must bear -
    Even so, and so only!

SERVICES

SHE was dead. Forth went the word,
And every creature heard.
To the last hamlet in the farthest lands,
To people countless as the sands
Of primal seas.
And with the word so sent
Her life's full record went, -

Of what fair line, how gifted, how endowed,
How educated; and then, told aloud,
The splendid tale of what her life had done;
And all the people heard and felt as one;
Exulting all together in their dead,
And the grand story of the life she led.

But in the city where her body lay
Great services were held on that fair day:
People by thousands; music to the sky;
Flowers of a garnered season; winding by,
Processions, glorious in rich array.
All massing in the temple where she lay.

Then, when the music rested, rose and stood
Those who could speak of her and count the good,
The measureless great good her life had spread,
That all might hear the praises of their dead.
And those who loved her sent from the world's end
Their tribute to the memory of their friend;
While teachers to their children whispered low,
"See that you have as many when you go!"

Then was recited how her life had part
In building up this science and that art,
Inventing here, administering there.
Helping to organize, create, prepare,
With fullest figures to expatiate
On her unmeasured value to the state.
And the child, listening, grew in noble pride,
And planned for greater praises when he died.
Then the Poet spoke of those long ripening years;
And tenderer music brought the grateful tears;

And then, lest grief upon their heartstrings hang,
Her children stood around the bier and sang:

In the name of the mother that bore us -
  Bore us strong - bore us free -
We will strive in the labors before us,
  Even as she! Even as she!

In the name of her wisdom and beauty,
  Of her life full of light.
We will live in our national duty,
  We will help on the right:

We will love as her heart loved before us,
  Warm and wide - strong and high!
In the name of the mother that bore us.
  We will live! We will die!

IN MOTHER-TIME

When woman looks at woman with the glory in
    her eyes,
When eternity lies open like a scroll,
When immortal life is being felt, - the life that
    never dies, -
  And the triumph of it ringeth
  And the sweetness of it singeth
      In the soul,

Then we come to California, the Garden of the
    Lord,

Through all its leagues of endless blossoming;
>   And we sing, we sing together, to the whole world's
>   deep accord -
>   And we feel each other praying
>   Over what the flowers are saying
>   As we sing.

We were waiting, we were growing, glad of heart
>   and strong of soul,
Like the peace and power of all these virgin lands;
Through the years of holy maidenhood with mother-
>   hood for goal -
>   And soon we shall be holding
>   Fruit of all life's glad unfolding
>   In our hands.

White-robed mothers, flower-crowned mothers, in
>   the splendor of their youth,
In the grandeur of maturity and power;
Feeling life has passed the telling in its joyousness
>   and truth,
>   Feeling life will soon be giving
>   Them the golden key of living
>   In one hour.

We come to California for the sunshine and the
>   flowers;
Our motherhood has brought us here as one;
For the fruit of all the ages should share the shining
>   hours,
>   With the blossoms ever-springing
>   And the golden globes low swinging,
>   In the sun.

SHE WHO IS TO COME

A WOMAN - in so far as she beholdeth
 Her one Beloved's face;
A mother - with a great heart that enfoldeth
 The children of the Race;
A body, free and strong, with that high beauty
 That comes of perfect use, is built thereof;
A mind where Reason ruleth over Duty,
 And Justice reigns with Love;
A self-poised, royal soul, brave, wise, and tender.
 No longer blind and dumb;
A Human Being, of an unknown splendor,
 Is she who is to come!

GIRLS OF TO-DAY

 Girls of to-day! Give ear!
Never since time began
Has come to the race of man
A year, a day, an hour,
So full of promise and power
 As the time that now is here!

 Never in all the lands
Was there a power so great,
To move the wheels of state,
To lift up body and mind,
To waken the deaf and blind.

As the power that is in your hands!

Here at the gates of gold
You stand in the pride of youth,
Strong in courage and truth.
Stirred by a force kept back
Through centuries long and black,
　Armed with a power threefold!

First: You are makers of men!
Then Be the things you preach!
Let your own greatness teach!
When mothers like this you see
Men will be strong and free -
　Then, and not till then!

Second: Since Adam fell,
Have you not heard it said
That men by women are led?
True is the saying - true!
See to it what you do!
　See that you lead them well!

Third: You have work of your own!
Maid and mother and wife,
Look in the face of life!
There are duties you owe the race!
Outside your dwelling-place
　There is work for you alone!

Maid and mother and wife,
See your own work be done!

Be worthy a noble son!
Help man in the upward way!
Truly, a girl to-day
  Is the strongest thing in life!

"WE, AS WOMEN"

There's a cry in the air about us -
  We hear it before, behind -
Of the way in which "We, as women,"
  Are going to lift mankind!'

With our white frocks starched and ruffled,
  And our soft hair brushed and curled -
Hats off! for "we, as women,"
  Are coming to help the world!
Fair sisters, listen one moment -
  And perhaps you'll pause for ten:
The business of women as women
  Is only with men as men!

What we do, "we, as women,"
  We have done all through our life;
The work that is ours as women
  Is the work of mother and wife!

But to elevate public opinion,
  And to lift up erring man,
Is the work of the Human Being;
  Let us do it - if we can.

But wait, warm-hearted sisters -
　　Not quite so fast, so far.
Tell me how we are going to lift a thing
　　Any higher than we are!

We are going to "purify politics"
　　And to "elevate the press."
We enter the foul paths of the world
　　To sweeten and cleanse and bless.

To hear the high things we are going to do,
　　And the horrors of man we tell.
One would think "we, as women," were angels,
　　And our brothers were fiends of hell.

We, that were born of one mother,
　　And reared in the selfsame place, -
In the school and the church together, -
　　We, of one blood, one race!

Now then, all forward together!
　　But remember, every one,
That it is not by feminine innocence
　　The work of the world is done.

The world needs strength and courage,
　　And wisdom to help and feed -
When "we, as women," bring these to man,
　　We shall lift the world indeed!

IF MOTHER KNEW

If mother knew the way I felt, -
    And I'm sure a mother should, -
She wouldn't make it quite so hard
    For a person to be good!
I want to do the way she says;
    I try to all day long;
And then she just skips all the right,
    And pounces on the wrong!

A dozen times I do a thing,
    And one time I forget;
And then she looks at me and asks
    If I can't remember yet?

She'll tell me to do something,
    And I'll really start to go;
But she'll keep right on telling it
    As if I didn't know.

Till it seems as if I couldn't -
    It makes me kind of wild;
And then she says she never saw
    Such a disobliging child.

I go to bed all sorry,
    And say my prayers, and cry,
And mean next day to be so good
    I just can't wait to try.

And I get up next morning,
    And mean to do just right;

But mother's sure to scold me
    About something, before night.

I wonder if she really thinks
    A child could go so far,
As to be perfect all the time
    As the grown up people are!

If she only knew I tried to, -
    And I 'm sure a mother should, -
She wouldn't make it quite so hard
    For a person to be good!

THE ANTI-SUFFRAGISTS

Fashionable women in luxurious homes,
With men to feed them, clothe them, pay their bills,
Bow, doff the hat, and fetch the handkerchief;
Hostess or guest, and always so supplied
With graceful deference and courtesy;
Surrounded by their servants, horses, dogs, -
These tell us they have all the rights they want.

Successful women who have won their way
Alone, with strength of their unaided arm,
Or helped by friends, or softly climbing up
By the sweet aid of "woman's influence;"
Successful any way, and caring naught
For any other woman's unsuccess, -
These tell us they have all the rights they want.

Religious women of the feebler sort, -
Not the religion of a righteous world,
A free, enlightened, upward-reaching world.
But the religion that considers life
As something to back out of! - whose ideal
Is to renounce, submit, and sacrifice,
Counting on being patted on the head
And given a high chair when they get to heaven, -
These tell us they have all the rights they want.

Ignorant women - college-bred sometimes,
But ignorant of life's realities
And principles of righteous government,
And how the privileges they enjoy
Were won with blood and tears by those before -
Those they condemn, whose ways they now oppose;
Saying, "Why not let well enough alone?
Our world is very pleasant as it is," -
These tell us they have all the rights they want.

And selfish women, - pigs in petticoats, -
Rich, poor, wise, unwise, top or bottom round,
But all sublimely innocent of thought.
And guiltless of ambition, save the one
Deep, voiceless aspiration - to be fed!
These have no use for rights or duties more.
Duties to-day are more than they can meet,
And law insures their right to clothes and food, -
These tell us they have all the rights they want.

And, more's the pity, some good women, too;
Good conscientious women, with ideas;

Who think - or think they think - that woman's
    cause
Is best advanced by letting it alone;
That she somehow is not a human thing,
And not to be helped on by human means,
Just added to humanity - an "L" -
A wing, a branch, an extra, not mankind, -
These tell us they have all the rights they want.

And out of these has come a monstrous thing,
A strange, down-sucking whirlpool of disgrace,
Women uniting against womanhood.
And using that great name to hide their sin!
Vain are their words as that old king's command
Who set his will against the rising tide.
But who shall measure the historic shame
Of these poor traitors - traitors are they all -
To great Democracy and Womanhood!

WOMEN DO NOT WANT IT

WHEN the woman suffrage argument first stood
    upon its legs,
They answered it with cabbages, they answered it
    with eggs,
They answered it with ridicule, they answered it
    with scorn,
They thought it a monstrosity that should not have
    been born.

When the woman suffrage argument grew vigorous
    and wise,
And was not to be silenced by these apposite
    replies,
They turned their opposition into reasoning severe
Upon the limitations of our God-appointed sphere.

We were told of disabilities, - a long array of these,
Till one would think that womanhood was merely
    a disease;
And "the maternal sacrifice" was added to the plan
Of the various sacrifices we have always made -
    to man.
Religionists and scientists, in amity and bliss,
However else they disagreed, could all agree on this,
And the gist of all their discourse, when you got
    down to it,
Was - we could not have the ballot because we
    were not fit!

They would not hear to reason, they would not
    fairly yield,
They would not own their arguments were beaten
    in the field;
But time passed on, and someway, we need not ask
    them how,
Whatever ails those arguments - we do not hear
    them now!

You may talk of woman suffrage now with an
    educated man,
And he agrees with all you say, as sweetly as he
    can;

'Twould be better for us all, of course, if womanhood was free;
But "the women do not want it" - and so it must
not be!

'T'is such a tender thoughtfulness! So exquisite
a care!
Not to pile on our fair shoulders what we do not
wish to bear!
But, oh, most generous brother! Let us look a little
more -
Have we women always wanted what you gave to
us before?

Did we ask for veils and harems in the Oriental
races?
Did we beseech to be "unclean," shut out of sacred
places?
Did we beg for scolding bridles and ducking stools
to come?
And clamor for the beating stick no thicker than
your thumb?

Did we seek to be forbidden from all the trades
that pay?
Did we claim the lower wages for a man's full work
to-day?
Have we petitioned for the laws wherein our shame
is shown:
That not a woman's child - nor her own body -
is her own?

What women want has never been a strongly act-
    ing cause
When woman has been wronged by man in churches,
    customs, laws;
Why should he find this preference so largely in
    his way
When he himself admits the right of what we ask
    to-day?

WEDDED BLISS

"O COME and be my mate!" said the Eagle to the
        Hen;
    "I love to soar, but then
    I want my mate to rest
    Forever in the nest!"
    Said the Hen, "I cannot fly,
    I have no wish to try,
But I joy to see my mate careering through the sky!"
They wed, and cried, "Ah, this is Love, my own!"
And the Hen sat, the Eagle soared, alone.

"O come and be my mate!" said the Lion to the
        Sheep;
    My love for you is deep!
    I slay, a Lion should,
    But you are mild and good!"
    Said the Sheep, "I do no ill -
    Could not, had I the will -
But I joy to see my mate pursue, devour, and kill."

They wed, and cried, "Ah, this is Love, my own!"
And the Sheep browsed, the Lion prowled, alone.

"O come and be my mate!" said the Salmon to the
            Clam;
    "You are not wise, but I am.
    I know sea and stream as well;
    You know nothing but your shell."
    Said the Clam, "I'm slow of motion,
    But my love is all devotion,
And I joy to have my mate traverse lake and stream
            and ocean!"
They wed, and cried, "Ah, this is Love, my own!"
And the Clam sucked, the Salmon swam, alone.

THE HOLY STOVE

O THE soap-vat is a common thing!
    The pickle-tub is low!
The loom and wheel have lost their grace
In falling from the dwelling-place
    To mills where all may go!
The bread-tray needeth not your love;
    The wash-tub wide doth roam;
Even the oven free may rove;
But bow ye down to the Holy Stove,
    The Altar of the Home!

Before it bend the worshippers,
    And wreaths of parsley twine;

Above it still the incense curls,
And a passing train of hired girls
     Do service at the shrine.
We toil to keep the altar crowned
     With dishes new and nice.
And Art and Love, and Time and Truth,
We offer up, with Health and Youth,
     In daily sacrifice.

Speak not to us of a fairer faith,
     Of a lifetime free from pain.
Our fathers always worshipped here,
Our mothers served this altar drear,
     And still we serve amain.
Our earliest dreams around it cling,
     Bright hopes that childhood sees,
And memory leaves a vista wide
Where Mother's Doughnuts rank beside
The thought of Mother's Knees.

The wood-box hath no sanctity;
     No glamour gilds the coal;
But the Cook-Stove is a sacred thing
To which a reverent faith we bring
     And serve with heart and soul.
The Home's a temple all divine,
     By the Poker and the Hod!
The Holy Stove is the altar fine,
The wife the priestess at the shrine -
     Now who can be the god?

THE MOTHER'S CHARGE

She raised her head. With hot and glittering eye,
"I know," she said, "that I am going to die.
Come here, my daughter, while my mind is clear.
Let me make plain to you your duty here;
My duty once - I never failed to try -
But for some reason I am going to die."
She raised her head, and, while her eyes rolled wild,
Poured these instructions on the gasping child:

"Begin at once - don't iron sitting down -
Wash your potatoes when the fat is brown -
Monday, unless it rains - it always pays
To get fall sewing done on the right days
A carpet-sweeper and a little broom -
Save dishes - wash the summer dining-room
With soda - keep the children out of doors -
The starch is out - beeswax on all the floors -
If girls are treated like your friends they stay -
They stay, and treat you like their friends - the way
To make home happy is to keep a jar -
And save the prettiest pieces for the star
In the middle - blue's too dark - all silk is best -
And don't forget the corners - when they're dressed
Put them on ice - and always wash the chest
Three times a day, the windows every week -
We need more flour - the bedroom ceilings leak -
It's better than onion - keep the boys at home -
Gardening is good - a load three loads of loam -
They bloom in spring - and smile, smile always,
    dear -
Be brave, keep on - I hope I've made it clear."

She died, as all her mothers died before.
Her daughter died in turn, and made one more.

A BROOD MARE

It is a significant fact that the phenomenal improvement in horses during recent years is accompanied by the growing conviction that good points and a good record are as desirable in the dam as in the sire, if not more so.

I HAD a quarrel yesterday,
    A violent dispute,
With a man who tried to sell to me
    A strange amorphous brute;

A creature disproportionate,
    A beast to make you stare,
An undeveloped, overgrown,
    Outrageous-looking mare.

Her fore legs they were weak and thin,
    Her hind legs weak and fat;
She was heavy in the quarters,
    With a narrow chest and flat;

And she had managed to combine -
    I'm sure I don't know how -
The barrel of a greyhound
    With the belly of a cow.

She seemed exceeding feeble.
    And he owned with manner bland
That she walked a little, easily,
    But wasn't fit to stand.

I tried to mount the animal
    To test her on the track;
But he cried in real anxiety,
    "Get off! You'll strain her back!"

And then I sought to harness her,
    But he explained at length
That any draught or carriage work
    Was quite beyond her strength.

"No use to carry or to pull!
    No use upon the course!"
Said I, "How can you have the face
    To call that thing a horse?"

Said he, indignantly, "I don't!
    I'm dealing on the square;
I never said it was a horse,
    I told you 't was a mare!

"A mare was never meant to race,
    To carry, or to pull;
She is meant for breeding only, so
    Her place in life is full."

Said I, "Do you pretend to breed
    From such a beast as that?

A mass of shapeless skin and bone,
Or shapeless skin and fat?"

Said he, "Her sire was thoroughbred,
As fine as walked the earth.
And all her colts receive from him
The marks of noble birth;

"And then I mate her carefully
With horses fine and fit;
Mares do not need to have themselves
The points which they transmit!"

Said I, "Do you pretend to say
You can raise colts as fair
From that fat cripple as you can
From an able-bodied mare?"

Quoth he, "I solemnly assert,
Just as I said before,
A mare that's good for breeding
Can be good for nothing more!"

Cried I, " One thing is certain proof;
One thing I want to see;
Trot out the noble colts you raise
From your anomaly."

He looked a little dashed at this,
And the poor mare hung her head.
"Fact is," said he, " she's had but one,
And that one - well, it's dead!"

FEMININE VANITY

FEMININE Vanity! O ye Gods! Hear to this man!
   As if silk and velvet and feathers and fur
   And jewels and gold had been just for her,
      Since the world began!

Where is his memory? Let him look back - all
     of the way!
   Let him study the history of his race
   From the first he-savage that painted his face
      To the dude of to-day!

Vanity! Oh! Are the twists and curls,
   The intricate patterns in red, black, and blue,
   The wearisome tortures of rich tattoo,
      Just made for girls?

Is it only the squaw who files the teeth,
   And dangles the lip, and bores the ear.
   And wears bracelet and necklet and anklet as
   queer
      As the bones beneath?

Look at the soldier, the noble, the king!
   Egypt or Greece or Rome discloses
   The purples and perfumes and gems and roses
     On a masculine thing!

Look at the men of our own dark ages!
   Heroes too, in their cloth of gold,
   With jewels as thick as the cloth could hold,
      On the knights and pages!

We wear false hair? Our man looks big!
But it's not so long, let me beg to state,
Since every gentleman shaved his pate
And wore a wig.

French heels Sharp toes? See our feet defaced?
But there was a day when the soldier free
Tied the toe of his shoe to the manly knee -
Yes, and even his waist!

We pad and stuff? Our man looks bolder.
Don't speak of the time when a bran-filled bunch
Made an English gentleman look like Punch -
But feel of his shoulder!

Feminine Vanity! O ye Gods! Hear to these men!
Vanity's wide as the world is wide!
Look at the peacock in his pride -
Is it a hen?'

THE MODEST MAID

I AM a modest San Francisco maid,
Fresh, fair, and young,
Such as the painters gladly have displayed,
The poets sung.

Modest? - Oh, modest as a bud unblown,
A thought unspoken;

Hidden and cherished, unbeheld, unknown,
 In peace unbroken.

Far from the holy shades of this my home,
 The coarse world raves.
And the New Woman cries to heaven's dome
 For what she craves.

Loud, vulgar, public, screaming from the stage,
 Her skirt divided.
Biding cross-saddled on the dying age,
 Justly derided.
I blush for her, I blush for our sweet sex
 By her disgraced.
My sphere is home. My soul I do not vex
 With zeal misplaced.

Come then to me with happy heart, O man!
 I wait your visit.
To guide your footsteps I do all I can,
 Am most explicit.

As veined flower - petals teach the passing bee
 The way to honey,
So printer's ink displayed instructeth thee
 Where lies my money.

Go see! In type and cut across the page,
 Before the nation,
There you may read about my eyes, my age.
 My education,
My fluffy golden hair, my tiny feet,

My pet ambition.
My well-developed figure, and my sweet,
Retiring disposition.

All, all is there, and now I coyly wait.
Pray don't delay.
My address does the Blue Book plainly state.
And mamma's "day."

UNSEXED

IT was a wild rebellious drone
That loudly did complain;
He wished he was a worker bee
With all his might and main.

"I want to work," the drone declared.
Quoth they, "The thing you mean
Is that you scorn to be a drone
And long to be a queen.

"You long to lay unnumbered eggs,
And rule the waiting throng;
You long to lead our summer flight.
And this is rankly wrong."

Cried he, "My life is pitiful!
I only eat and wed,
And in my marriage is the end -

Thereafter I am dead.
"I would I were the busy bee
    That flits from flower to flower;
I long to share in work and care
    And feel the worker's power."

Quoth they, "The life you dare to spurn
    Is set before you here
As your one great, prescribed, ordained,
    Divinely ordered sphere!

"Without your services as drone.
    We should not be alive;
Your modest task, when well fulfilled,
    Preserves the busy hive.

"Why underrate your blessed power?
    Why leave your rightful throne
To choose a field of life that's made
    For working bees alone?"

Cried he, "But it is not enough,
    My momentary task!
Let me do that and more beside:
    To work is all I ask!"

Then fiercely rose the workers all,
    For sorely were they vexed
"O wretch!" they cried, "should this betide,
    You would become *unsexed!*"
And yet he had not sighed for eggs,
    Nor yet for royal mien;

He longed to be a worker bee,
    But not to be a queen.

FEMALES

The female fox she is a fox;
    The female whale a whale;
The female eagle holds her place
As representative of race
    As truly as the male.

The mother hen doth scratch for her chicks,
    And scratch for herself beside;
The mother cow doth nurse her calf,
Yet fares as well as her other half
    In the pasture free and wide.

The female bird doth soar in air;
    The female fish doth swim;
The fleet-foot mare upon the course
Doth hold her own with the flying horse -
    Yea, and she beateth him!

One female in the world we find
    Telling a different tale.
It is the female of our race,
Who holds a parasitic place
    Dependent on the male.
Not so, saith she, ye slander me!

No parasite am I!
I earn my living as a wife;
My children take my very life.
 Why should I share in human strife.
 To plant and build and buy?

The human race holds highest place
 In all the world so wide,
Yet these inferior females wive,
 And raise their little ones alive,
 And feed themselves beside.

The race is higher than the sex,
 Though sex be fair and good;
A Human Creature is your state.
And to be human is more great
 Than even womanhood!

The female fox she is a fox;
 The female whale a whale;
The female eagle holds her place
As representative of race
 As truly as the male.

A MOTHER'S SOLILOQUY

You soft, pink, moving thing!
Young limbs that crave
Motion as free as zephyr-lifted wave
Uneasy with the push of unlearned powers!

Exploring slowly through half-conscious hours;
With what rich new surprise and joy you feel
Your own will move yourself from head to heel!
So, let me swaddle you in bandage tight,
Dress you in wide, confining folds of white,
Cover you warmly, hold you close, and so
A mother's instinct-guided love I'll show!

Mysterious little frame!
Each organ new
And learning swiftly what it has to do!
Thy life's bright stream - as yet so newly thine -
Refreshed by heaven's sunlit air divine;
With what delight you breathe in rosy ease
The strengthening, restful, blossom-scented breeze!
So, let me wrap you in a blanket shawl,
And veil your face in woollen, when at all
You meet the air. Here in my arms is best
The curtained bedroom where your elders rest;
So shall I guard you from a draught, and so
A mother's instinct-guided love I'll show.

Young earnest mind at work!
Each sense attends
To teach you life's approaching foes and friends;
Eye, ear, nose, tongue, and ever ready hand,
Eager to help you learn and understand.
What floods of happiness the day insures,
While each new knowledge is becoming yours!
So, let me firmly take away from you
The things you so persistently would view;
And when you stretch the hand that tells so much,

Rap your soft knuckles and exclaim, " Don't touch!"
I'll tell you what you ought to learn, and so,
A mother's instinct-guided love I'll show.

An ordinary child at best,
So neighbors tell;
Not very large and strong, not very well;
A victim to the measles and the croup,
Fevers that flush and chill, and coughs that whoop;
To unknown naughtiness and well-known pain;
No racial progress here - no special gain!
But I, your mother, see with other eyes;
I hold you second to none under skies.
This estimate, unbased on any fact.
Shall teach you how to feel and how to act,
Shall make you wise, and true. and strong, and so,
A mother's instinct-guided love I'll show.

THEY WANDERED FORTH

THEY wandered forth in springtime woods,
    Three women, thickly hung
With yards and yards of woollen goods -
    To play that they were young!

The river raced with the racing air;
    The woods were wild with song;
The glad birds darted everywhere -
    And so they walked along!

Stiff-bodied, fat, oppressed with cloth,
  Dull-colored, sad to see,
Slow-moving over the bright grass,
  Their shapeless shadows fall and pass,
And dreaming not - alas! alas!
  Of what dear life might be!

BABY LOVE

BABY LOVE came prancing by,
Cap on head and sword on thigh,
Horse to ride and drum to beat, -
All the world beneath his feet.

Mother Life was sitting there,
Hard at work and full of care,
Set of mouth and sad of eye.
Baby Love came prancing by.

Baby Love was very proud,
Very lively, very loud;
Mother Life arose in wrath,
Set an arm across his path.

Baby Love wept loud and long,
But his mother's arm was strong.
Mother had to work, she said.
Baby Love was put to bed.

Other Books by Charlotte Perkins Gilman
published by **Aziloth Books**

THE HERLAND TRILOGY

Charlotte Perkins Gilman was an American sociologist, poet, novelist, and activist for gender equality and social reform. Her most famous work today is the semi-autobiographical, The Yellow Wallpaper, (also published by Aziloth Books), but arguably more important is Gilman's fictional 'Herland Trilogy'. Universally recognized as a classic of early feminist literature, the books recount the utopian advances made in 'Herland' - a parthenogenetic all-female society isolated from the rest of humanity for 2000 years - and the disruption caused by the arrival of three male American adventurers.

Moving The Mountain

Moving the Mountain was published in Gilman's magazine The Forerunner in 1911, and appeared in book form later that same year. It tells the tale of American John Robertson, a native of South Carolina, and student of ancient languages, who at the age of 25 travels to Tibet and, after an unfortunate accident, suffers complete memory loss. Thirty years later, in 1940, he is found by his sister Nellie, recovers his memory and returns to the United States.

Much has altered since John left his native shore. Women have become emancipated and have changed many aspects of society for the better: crime, poverty, prostitution, corruption and racism are no more. For John the culture shock is extreme – he retains the misogynist world-view of his youth, and finds equality of the sexes a bitter pill to swallow. Gilman skillfully uses John's (fictional) reactionary feelings to dissect and reject the (actual) domination and gender discrimination practiced by the men of her own time. A timely reminder of how far feminism has come – and altered - in the past 100 years.

Herland

Charlotte Perkins Gilman was known as a crusading feminist intellectual, concerned especially with gender inequality within marriage. Most married women of her time had little chance of participating in any creative or professional career – an enforced domestic slavery that was, for Gilman, not only patently unjust, but made neither partner happy or content.

In Herland, Gilman weaves these themes into an adventure story of three young men, schooled in the then-current view of women as weak and timid creatures. They discover Herland, an all-female society of rationality, equality and compassion composed solely of strong, athletic women, where even reproduction requires no male input. Gilman uses this utopian fantasy with skill and humour, gradually bringing the three male adventurers from an initial arrogant confidence in their own culture, to a realization that life in Herland is infinitely preferable to the war-torn, poverty-stricken male-dominated nations they have left. And that the supposed inferiority of the weaker sex is, in fact, nothing more than a product of cultural indoctrination.

With Her In Ourland

With Her in Ourland is the third and final installment of the saga, and has Herlander Ellador, now married (platonically) to Vandyck Jennings, leaving her home and engaging in a tour of 'Ourland' - the rest of the world. Ellador's calm, logical responses to the problems of war, poverty, misogyny, racial prejudice and other worldly evils, allow Gilman to continue her satirical, dystopian critique of the so-called civilized world, with husband Vandyck's complacent acceptance of worldly injustice acting as the perfect foil to Ellador/Gilman's prescriptions for setting the place to rights. The result is a tour de force of Charlotte Gilman's wit and political perception, making for an astute and distinctly prescient account of both our past, and present-day, problems.

AZILOTH ||| BOOKS

Aziloth Books publishes a wide range of titles ranging from hard-to-find esoteric books - *Parchment Books* - to classic works on fiction, politics and philosophy - *Cathedral Classics*. Our newest venture is *Aziloth Books Children's Classics*, with vibrant new covers and illustrations to complement some of the world's very best children's tales. All our imprints are offered to the reader at a competitive price and through as many mediums and outlets as possible.

We are committed to excellent book production and strive, whenever possible, to add value to our titles with original images, maps and author introductions. With the premium on space in most modern dwellings, we also endeavour - within the limits of good book design - to make our products as slender as possible, allowing more books to be fitted into a given bookshelf area.

We are a small, approachable company and would love to hear any of your comments and suggestions on our plans, products, or indeed on absolutely anything.

Aziloth Books is also interested in hearing from aspiring authors whom we might publish. We look forward to meeting you.

Contact us at: info@azilothbooks.com.

CATHEDRAL CLASSICS

Cathedral Classics hosts an array of classic literature, from erudite ancient tomes to avant-garde, twentieth-century masterpieces, all of which deserve a place in your home. All the world's great novelists are here, Jane Austen, Dickens, Conrad, Arthur Machen and Henry James, brushing shoulders with such disparate luminaries as Sun Tzu, Marcus Aurelius, Kipling, Friedrich Nietzsche, Machiavelli, and Omar Khayam. A small selection is detailed below:

Frankenstein	Mary Shelley
The Time Machine; The Invisible Man	H. G. Wells
The Prince	Niccolo Machiavelli
The Rubaiyat of Omar Khayyam	Omar Khayyam
Heart of Darkness; The Secret Agent	Joseph Conrad
Persuasion; Northanger Abbey	Jane Austen
The Picture of Dorian Gray	Oscar Wilde
Candide	Voltaire
The Coming Race	Bulwer Lytton
The Adventures of Sherlock Holmes	Arthur Conan Doyle
The Thirty-Nine Steps	John Buchan
Beyond Good and Evil	Friedrich Nietzsche
Washington Square	Henry James
The Red Badge of Courage	Stephen Crane
Self-Reliance, & Other Essays (series 1&2)	Ralph W. Emmerson
The Art of War	Sun Tzu
A Christmas Carol	Charles Dicken
The Gambler; The Double	Fyodor Dostoyevsky
To the Lighthouse; Mrs Dalloway	Virginia Wolf
The Sorrows of Young Werther	Johann W. Goethe
Leaves of Grass - 1855 edition	Walt Whitman
Analects	Confucius
Beowulf	Anonymous
Agnes Grey	Anne Bronte
Utopia	Thomas More

Obtainable at all good online and local bookstores.
View Aziloth Books' full list at: www.azilothbooks.com

PARCHMENT BOOKS

Parchment Books enshrines the concept of the oneness of all true religious traditions - that "the light shines from many different lanterns". Our list below offers titles from both eastern and western spiritual traditions, including Christian, Judaic, Islamic, Daoist, Hindu and Buddhist mystical texts, as well as books on alchemy, hermeticism, paganism, etc..

By bringing together such spiritual texts, we hope to make esoteric and occult knowledge more readily available to those ready to receive it. We do not publish grimoires or any titles pertaining to the left hand path. Titles include:

Abandonment to Divine Providence	Jean-Pierre de Caussade
Corpus Hermeticum	G.R. S. Mead (trans.)
The Holy Rule of St Benedict	St. Benedict of Nursia
The Way of Perfection	St. Teresa of Avila
The Cloud Upon the Sanctuary	Karl von Eckhartshausen
The Confession of St Patrick	St. Patrick
The Outline of Sanity	G K Chesterton
The Dialogue Of St Catherine Of Siena	St. Catherine of Siena
Esoteric Christianity	Annie Besant
The Spiritual Exercises of St. Ignatius	St. Ignatius of Loyola
Dark Night of the Soul	St. John of the Cross
The Gospel of Thomas	Anonymous
St. Francis	G K Chesterton
The Imitation of Christ	Thomas à Kempis
The Interior Castle	St. Teresa of Avila
Songs of Innocence & Experience	William Blake
The Marriage of Heaven & Hell	William Blake
The Secret of the Rosary	St. Louis Marie de Montfort
Tertium Organum	P.D. Ouspensky
From Ritual to Romance	Jessie L. Weston
Kundalini	G. S. Arundale
The God of the Witches	Margaret Murray

Obtainable at all good online and local bookstores.
View Aziloth Books' full list at: www.azilothbooks.com

AZILOTH BOOKS CHILDREN'S CLASSICS

Aziloth Books is passionate about bringing the very best in children's classics fiction to the next generation of book-lovers. Renowned for its original design and outstanding quality, our highly successful list has something to suit every age and interest. Titles include:

The Railway Children	Edith Nesbit
5 Children and It	Edith Nesbit
Anne of Green Gables	Lucy Maud Montgomery
What Katy Did	Susan Coolidge
What Katy Did Next	Susan Coolidge
Puck of Pook's Hill	Rudyard Kipling
The Jungle Books	Rudyard Kipling
Just So Stories	Rudyard Kipling
Alice Through the Looking Glass	Charles Dodgson
Alice's Adventures in Wonderland	Charles Dodgson
Black Beauty	Anna Sewell
The War of the Worlds	H. G Wells
The Time Machine	H. G .Wells
The Sleeper Awakes	H. G. Wells
The Invisible Man	H. G. Wells
Treasure Island	Robert Louis Stevenson
Dr Jekyll and Mr Hyde	Robert Louis Stevenson
Kidnapped	Robert Louis Stevenson
Catriona (David Balfour)	Robert Louis Stevenson
The Water Babies	Charles Kingsley
The First Men in the Moon	Jules Verne
The Lost World	Sir Arthur Conan Doyle
A Christmas Carol	Charles Dickens
Call of the Wild	Jack London
Greenmantle	John Buchan
The Secret Garden	Frances Hodgson Burnett
A Little Princess	Frances Hodgson Burnett
Peter Pan	J. M. Barrie

Obtainable at all good online and local bookstores.
View Aziloth Books' full list at: www.azilothbooks.com

www.ingramcontent.com/pod-product-compliance
Lightning Source LLC
Chambersburg PA
CBHW071716140626
46557CB00011B/728